"B" Is for Betsy

BOOKS BY CAROLYN HAYWOOD

"B" Is for Betsy
Betsy and Billy
Back to School with Betsy
Betsy and the Boys

Here's a Penny
Penny and Peter
Primrose Day
Two and Two Are Four

"B" Is for Betsy

Carolyn Haywood

Illustrated by the author

AN ODYSSEY/HARCOURT YOUNG CLASSIC

HARCOURT, INC.

Orlando   Austin   New York   San Diego   Toronto   London

www.HarcourtBooks.com

First Harcourt Young Classics edition 2004
First Odyssey Classics edition 1990
First published 1939

Library of Congress Cataloging-in-Publication Data
Haywood, Carolyn, 1898–
"B" is for Betsy/Carolyn Haywood.
p.   cm.
"An Odyssey/Harcourt Young Classic."
Sequel: Betsy and Billy.
Summary: Betsy experiences an interesting first year in school
and looks forward to summer vacation at her grandfather's farm.
[1. Schools—Fiction.]   I. Title.
PZ7.H31496Bab   2004
[Fic]—dc22   2003056567
ISBN 0-15-205103-1   ISBN 0-15-205099-X (pb)

Printed in the United States of America

A C E G H F D B
C E G H F D   (pb)

*To my friend
who owns Koala Bear
this book is
lovingly inscribed*

CONTENTS

"B" Is for Betsy

1

Betsy Goes to School and Finds a Big Surprise

Betsy lay in her little white bed. She had been awake a long time. Outside her window the birds were calling "Good morning" to each other, but Betsy did not hear them.

All summer long she had jumped out of bed as soon as her eyes were open. She had always run to the window and thrown sunflower seeds out to the birds for their breakfast. But this morning Betsy was so busy feeling unhappy that she forgot all about the birds.

Betsy was unhappy because today was the first day of school. She had never been to school and she was sure she would not like it. Old Ned, who cut the grass on Grandfather's farm, had told her all about school. Betsy had never told anyone what Old Ned had told her, but now she lay thinking about it. She thought of the cross old teacher and of the switch that had stood in the corner to be used on the legs of any child who might be late for school. She thought of the high pointed cap made of paper that Old Ned had been made to wear when he didn't know his spelling. Old Ned had stroked his grizzly beard and said, "Aye, yes! School was a terrible place."

Betsy turned her head on the pillow. Now she could see her clothes lying on her bedroom chair. There was her new green dress with the little puffy pockets. It was such a pretty dress but Betsy wished that she did not have to go to school in it. She leaned far over the side of her bed to see if she could see her new shoes. There they were, side by side, little brown shoes that fastened with a strap and a brass buckle. And there, hanging on the doorknob, was her schoolbag. It

was dark green with red and yellow stripes running up and down and across it. Mother called
it plaid. It was trimmed with bright red and there
was a long leather strap that Betsy could hang
over her shoulder. Betsy had been happy the
day Father had bought the bag for her. But now
that the time had come for her to wear it she
didn't feel happy at all. If only she could run
away and hide!

Just then Mother came in. "Come, Betsy, it's
time to get up," said Mother. "Today you are
going to school."

Mother helped her with her bath and brushed and braided her hair. Then she tied the crisp white sash on her dress.

After breakfast, Mother went upstairs to put on her hat. She was going to walk to school with Betsy every morning until Betsy knew the way.

Betsy sat on the bottom step of the stairs to wait for Mother. Her schoolbag was over her shoulder. There were two bread and jelly sandwiches tucked away in the pocket on the outside of the bag. Betsy felt very little and very scared, but she wouldn't tell Mother, because she did not want Mother to think that she was a baby. Only that morning Mother had called her "Mother's great big girl."

Suddenly Betsy thought of Koala Bear. Koala was the little toy bear that Uncle Jim had brought all the way from Australia. She would take Koala to school with her. It would not seem so strange or so lonely with Koala. Betsy ran upstairs and into her bedroom. She looked in the bed, but Koala was not there. Betsy was sure she had taken him to bed with her the night before. She pulled up the covers at the foot of the bed, for although Koala always went to bed with his nose sticking out at the top, it was nearly always

4

sticking out at the bottom of the bed in the morning. Sometimes he even fell out completely. Betsy looked under the bed and around the floor, but there was no Koala. She looked on the window-sill and in the toy closet, but Koala was nowhere to be seen.

"Betsy," called Mother from the foot of the stairs, "come at once, dear. You mustn't be late for school."

Betsy took one last look in the bed, but there was no sign of a little gray bear. Very slowly she went downstairs.

"I can't find Koala, Mother," said Betsy.

"Well, never mind Koala now," replied Mother. "He'll turn up; he always does."

Betsy took hold of Mother's hand, and they started on the long walk to school. Mother took such big long steps that Betsy had to take little skipping steps to keep up with her. Every time she skipped she could hear her two pencils rattle in the pencil box inside her schoolbag.

As they drew near the school, they saw a great many little boys and girls. They were coming from all directions. Some were with their mothers. Others were with big brothers and sisters. Betsy wondered whether all of the new little boys and girls were as frightened as she was.

At last they reached the school. Up the wide stone steps went Betsy, holding tightly to Mother's hand. In a little room a lady wearing glasses wrote Betsy's name on a pink card.

"Come this way, Betsy," said the lady with the glasses. She opened a door and Mother and Betsy passed into a room full of boys and girls. Each one was sitting behind a little brown desk.

A young lady with pale yellow hair shook hands with Mother. "This is Miss Grey, who will be Betsy's teacher," said the lady with the glasses.

"Good morning, Betsy," said Miss Grey.

"Good morning," said Betsy, as Mother quietly slipped out the door.

Betsy was alone now in a strange new place. What a big room it was! One whole side of the room was made of windows. They were the biggest windows Betsy had ever seen. The walls seemed so far away and parts of them were black. In some places there was writing on the black walls. And the ceiling—how high it was! It looked way, way off. So this was school! This great big room with the black walls and all the little desks was school. This was where she would have to come every morning. Betsy blinked her eyes to keep back the tears.

Miss Grey led her to a desk by the windows. It seemed such a long way from the door to the little desk. It seemed much longer than the whole way she had walked with Mother.

"This will be your desk, Betsy," said Miss Grey.

Betsy took off her schoolbag and sat down. She thought of Mother who was getting farther and farther away every moment. *If I got up now and ran out the door*, thought Betsy, *I could catch Mother. I could be out in the sunshine again with Mother and take hold of her hand. I could*

*tell Mother that I don't want to go to school, that
I know it is a terrible place, Old Ned said so.*
But Betsy knew that she couldn't do that. She
knew that Mother would bring her back again
and would be ashamed of her. Nothing could be
done about it. She would have to stay. Two big
tears began to roll down Betsy's cheeks. She felt
in her pocket for her handkerchief. It was not
there. Then Betsy remembered that Mother had
put it in her schoolbag. Betsy opened the bag
and took out her shiny black pencil box. She
felt for her handkerchief. As she did so, her

hand touched something soft and furry. Betsy looked inside the bag and there, looking at her with bright beady eyes, was Koala Bear. Tied around his neck was one of Father's old red neckties, so Betsy knew that Father must have hidden Koala in her schoolbag. Betsy wanted to hug him up tight, but instead she just put her hand in the bag and gave Koala a little squeeze and whispered, "Oh, Koala! I'm so glad to see you."

Betsy was so surprised to see Koala that she forgot all about her handkerchief and when she did think of it she found that she didn't need it after all.

2

How Betsy Found Ellen

Betsy looked down at the lid of her little brown desk. It was so new and shiny that Betsy could see her face and the two red ribbons on the ends of her braids. Betsy thought of Koala, safely tucked away in her schoolbag under the lid. It was nice to know that he was so near.

She lifted her eyes and looked around her. Miss Grey was showing another little girl to a desk near the door. "This will be your desk, Ellen," Betsy heard Miss Grey say.

Betsy looked at her teacher. Miss Grey's pale yellow hair and big blue eyes made Betsy think of her very best doll, Judith. Betsy knew that she could never be afraid of someone who looked just like her best doll.

Then Betsy thought of the switch. Old Ned had said that it always hung in the corner. She looked in the nearest corner. There was nothing there but a large patch of bright sunshine. She looked in the corner by the door. There was a little table with a big bowl filled with goldenrod. *Perhaps*, thought Betsy, *it hangs in the back of the room.* Very slowly she turned her head and looked behind her. The corner was filled with a big sand table. She turned again and looked in the far corner. There, hanging from a big hook, was a long string of brightly painted fruit—apples, oranges, lemons, and bananas. They were gayer than any Betsy had ever seen before. *Old Ned must have been wrong*, thought Betsy, *for there isn't any switch at all.*

Just then a loud bell rang. It made Betsy jump. "That bell," said Miss Grey, "tells us that it is nine o'clock and that school must begin.

The nicest way to begin," she added, "is with a song. I wonder if anyone here knows a 'Good-morning Song'?"

Now Betsy knew a "Good-morning Song." Mother had taught it to her and she often sang it to the little birds who came to her window for sunflower seeds.

Miss Grey was looking right at Betsy. "Do you know a 'Good-morning Song,' Betsy?" asked Miss Grey.

"I know a little one," replied Betsy.

"Well, Betsy," said Miss Grey, "will you come up to the front of the room and sing your 'Good-morning Song' for us?"

Betsy walked to the front of the room and this is the song she sang—

> "Good morning," chirped the robin,
> "Good morning," buzzed the bee,
> "The sun is shining brightly,
> Wake up," they called to me.

"Now," said Miss Grey, "let's all try to sing the song." And because it was a very easy song all of the boys and girls were able to sing the song with Betsy.

Betsy returned to her seat and Miss Grey began to tell the children a story about a little speckled hen. Suddenly there was a sharp bark, "Bow! Wow!," and a scratching noise on the door. Miss Grey went to the door and opened it. Into the room dashed a great big police dog. He flew straight to the little girl named Ellen. With happy yelps, he jumped up and licked her face. "Oh, Jerry, where did you come from?" cried Ellen. All the children stood up to see the big dog.

"Is he your dog, Ellen?" asked Miss Grey.

"Yes, Miss Grey," said Ellen, "he must have followed me."

"Well, you must send him home, Ellen," said Miss Grey.

"I think he would be good if he could stay," said Ellen.

"No," replied Miss Grey, "we can't have dogs in school."

Ellen took the big dog by his collar and led him to the door. "Go home, Jerry," she said, as she put him outside.

"Arf! Arf!" barked Jerry as soon as the door was closed. He began to scratch on the door harder than before. "Arf! Arf! Arf!" he barked. Scratch, scratch, scratch!

Miss Grey went to the door again. She opened it just a little, but Jerry pushed through. Again he ran to Ellen. He jumped up and down, wildly. The children laughed at Ellen's dog.

"Ellen," said Miss Grey, "I will have to send for your brother. He will have to take the dog home." So Miss Grey sent one of the little boys up to the sixth grade to get Ellen's big brother, Teddy.

In a few moments Teddy arrived. When he saw the dog, who was now lying at Ellen's feet, he said, "Here, Jerry. Come on, Jerry," but Jerry wouldn't budge.

"Go on, Jerry," said Ellen. "Go with Teddy." Jerry just rolled his big eyes.

"Come, Jerry," said Teddy, as he walked over to the dog. Jerry gave a low growl. Teddy put out his hand to take the dog by the collar. Jerry growled louder. "Oh, Jerry," said Ellen, "don't be a naughty boy; go home with Teddy." Jerry just lay with his head on his paws.

Teddy spoke quietly to Miss Grey. Betsy heard him say something about a butcher shop on the corner. Miss Grey nodded her head and Teddy went out of the room. All of the children crowded around Ellen to look at Jerry. Some of the little

boys said, "Come on, Jerry, come on," but Jerry lay like a rock at Ellen's feet and rolled his eyes from one child to the other.

In a few minutes Teddy opened the door. "Here, Jerry," he cried, and he held up a big bone. Jerry jumped up and dashed to the door. "I'll lead him home with it and then I'll give it to him," said Teddy as he closed the door.

Miss Grey and all of the children laughed, but Ellen looked just a little sad.

"Now," said Miss Grey, "I will go on with the story about the little speckled hen." But before she could finish the story the bell rang for recess.

The doors of the school opened, filling the schoolyard with boys and girls. Betsy, with her schoolbag over her shoulder, ran to the iron fence. She opened her bag and took out Koala. She rested her cheek against his furry body. It was so good to have Koala!

Betsy stepped up on the lowest rail in the iron fence. Holding tightly to the fence with one hand she could see over the heads of all the children and see what was going on all over the school-yard. Nearby there was a drinking fountain. It was surrounded with little boys who pushed and shoved. Now they were off, shouting and chasing

each other. The water bubbled up invitingly. Betsy saw Ellen run toward the fountain. At the same time two big boys came racing through the yard around the fountain, and with a bump, right into little Ellen. Ellen tumbled to the ground. The boys rushed on.

Ellen picked herself up. Sitting down on a nearby step, she put her head on her arms and wept.

Betsy walked over to the step and sat down beside Ellen.

"You didn't hurt yourself, did you?" asked Betsy.

Ellen shook her head and went on crying.

"Don't cry," said Betsy, leaning over Ellen's red curly head.

"I don't like school," sobbed Ellen. "I want to go home to Jerry."

"Would you like to hold Koala?" asked Betsy, very gently.

Ellen looked out with one eye, between two fingers. "Who is Koala?" asked Ellen.

"He is my bear from Australia," said Betsy, holding Koala out to Ellen.

Ellen took him in her arms. "He's nice, isn't he?" said she, her face still wet with tears.

Just then Betsy remembered her bread and jelly sandwiches. She opened the pocket of her schoolbag and pulled out the little package. Betsy gave one of the sandwiches to Ellen and the two little girls sat side by side eating them and talking of Koala.

When recess was over they tucked Koala back into Betsy's schoolbag and hand in hand ran to their classroom.

When the day was over and it was time to go home, Ellen called, "Good-bye, Betsy"; and Betsy said, "Good-bye, Ellen, I'll see you tomorrow."

As Betsy went down the steps of the school

she saw Mother waiting for her by the school-yard gate. Betsy rushed to her.

"Did you have a happy day, dear?" asked Mother.

"Mother," said Betsy, "I have a friend. Her name is Ellen."

3

How Betsy Went to School Alone

E very day during September Mother had walked to school with Betsy. Every night when Betsy went to bed she would say, "Pretty soon I will be able to go to school by myself." She was certain now that she knew the way. You walked to the corner and followed the cartracks to the railroad station. You went under the bridge and turned right on the second street. Then you went on until you came to the big, wide street where Mr. Kilpatrick stood.

Mr. Kilpatrick was the policeman who took the children across the street before and after school. He was a big man with a merry, red face and he loved little boys and girls. He would blow his sharp whistle and all the automobiles and wagons would stop. Then he would gather a group of boys and girls around him, and, like a hen with her chickens, hurry them across the wide street. "Hurry up, Bobby," he would say. "Mind you get a hundred today, Bill. Come along, Betty Lou, pick up your feet; sure I can't keep the traffic waiting all day."

Mr. Kilpatrick's bright red police car was always parked near the corner. Betsy thought it was a beautiful car. It was so red and shiny. Father's automobile was black and only the wheels were red. She wished that Father was a policeman; then she could ride in an automobile that was all red.

One morning, when Mother and Betsy were crossing the street, Mr. Kilpatrick called out, "Good morning, Little Red Ribbons; sure that's a pretty plaid schoolbag you've got over your shoulder."

Betsy liked Mr. Kilpatrick. She looked forward to seeing him every morning and every afternoon. Rain or shine he was always there. Mother told Betsy that she must never, never cross the wide street without Mr. Kilpatrick, and Betsy said she never would.

One evening, Betsy said, "Mother, I am sure I can go to school alone now. I know the way."

"Very well," said Mother. "You may go alone tomorrow."

Betsy felt very big indeed as she walked out of her front gate alone the following morning. Mother stood at the door and watched Betsy go up the street. When she reached the corner she looked back and waved her hand. Mother threw her a kiss.

Betsy followed the cartracks. After she passed the turn in the road, she could see the railroad bridge by the station. It was easy to go to school alone, thought Betsy. She walked along as quickly as her short little legs could carry her. Sometimes she skipped and her schoolbag bounced up and down.

As she passed the flower shop, she stopped to look in the window. Betsy loved flowers and these were beautiful. Soon she was so busy choosing the flowers she liked best that she forgot Mother had told her never to look in the shop windows on the way to school because she might look too long and be late. When she remembered Mother's warning, Betsy began to run. It would be dreadful to be late the very first morning that Mother had let her go alone! Now she was at the railroad station. Under the bridge and around the corner she ran. Soon she would reach Mr. Kilpatrick. She was out of breath from running. She would have to walk for a while. Betsy trotted along.

It was strange not to see any other children. She usually saw them after she passed the railroad station. Perhaps they were already in school. Betsy began to run again. Everything looked strange. She didn't remember this big open field.

Where, oh, where were the wide street and Mr. Kilpatrick! Perhaps he would be gone when she got there and how would she ever get across alone? *Oh, why did I stop to look at those flowers?* thought Betsy.

She wanted to cry, but she knew that it wouldn't help a bit; so she hurried on. There were some little houses in the next block. She could see a large lady sweeping the pavement. *Perhaps she could tell me how to get to school,* thought Betsy. Betsy remembered that Mother had told her never to speak to anyone on the street but a policeman, but there was no policeman.

When Betsy reached the lady with the broom, the lady stopped sweeping. She leaned on her broom and looked down at Betsy. "Well, darlin'," said the lady, "and where are you goin' this bright mornin'?"

"I'm going to school," said Betsy, "but I can't find it. I'm all mixed up."

"Well, sure," said the lady, "you're way off. You must have taken the wrong turn."

Tears came into Betsy's eyes.

"Now don't you fret," said the lady. "It will be all right. If it weren't for my feet bein' that bad, I'd take you myself. But my Patrick will be here soon, for it's nine o'clock and he'll be

wantin' his breakfast. Patrick will have you there in a jiffy. Come sit on the porch step and wait for him," said the lady.

She opened the front gate, and Betsy went into the little yard and sat down on the porch step. It was a pretty yard with chrysanthemums growing all along the fence and borders of petunias. "And now while we're waiting for Patrick, I'll pick some flowers for your teacher. It will help her to feel a mite better about you bein' late for school."

Betsy watched her pick the chrysanthemums. She had gathered a large bunch when a bright red police car drove up and stopped in front of the house. "Here's Patrick now," said the lady.

The door of the car opened and out stepped Mr. Kilpatrick. Betsy rushed to meet him. "Well, if it isn't Little Red Ribbons," cried Mr. Kilpatrick.

"Oh, Mr. Kilpatrick," cried Betsy, "I got lost going to school. I couldn't find you, Mr. Kilpatrick."

"Well, sure it's good you found my wife, Katie," said Mr. Kilpatrick, picking Betsy up in his big strong arms.

"And now, Pat, run her over to the school

and hurry back for your breakfast," said Mrs. Kilpatrick.

Mr. Kilpatrick put Betsy in his bright red automobile and his wife gave her the big bunch of chrysanthemums. Mr. Kilpatrick climbed into the driver's seat and in no time at all they reached Betsy's school.

"I'll take you into your room," said Mr. Kilpatrick.

"Oh, thank you," said Betsy.

Betsy was glad to have him go into the room with her, for she didn't like to go alone. When Mr. Kilpatrick opened the door and Betsy walked into the room, all the children called out, "Here's Betsy," and some of the little boys called out, "Hello, Mr. Kilpatrick."

Miss Grey said, "Why, Betsy, I am so glad to see you. We were wondering where you were."

"I'm sorry I got lost," said Betsy as she handed the big bunch of chrysanthemums to her teacher. "Mrs. Kilpatrick said they would make you feel a mite better about my being late," she added.

Miss Grey laughed and said, "Oh, they do, Betsy; they do."

"Miss Grey," said Betsy, "I rode in Mr. Kilpatrick's red police car."

4

How Wiggle and Waggle Grew Up

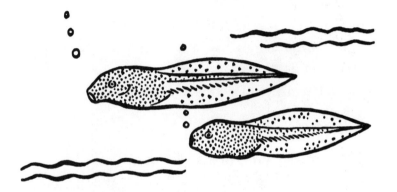

One morning when Betsy was walking to school, she saw Billy Porter trotting along ahead of her. Billy was also in the first grade, and his desk was right near Betsy's. Billy was a pudgy little boy with a round, merry face. He had thick, bushy, brown hair that stood up all over his head. It looked as though it had been cut with a lawn mower. Billy was carrying a cardboard box by its wire handle. One by one little drops of water were dropping from the bottom of the box.

"What's in the box?" asked Betsy, as she caught up to Billy.

Billy grinned. "Oh, wait 'til you see," said Billy. He set the box down on the pavement and opened the lid. Betsy stooped down and looked in the box. It was filled with water. Swimming in the water were what looked like two little gray fish.

"What are you going to do with those fish?" asked Betsy.

"They're not fish," said Billy, "they're tadpoles. I am going to give them to the teacher."

"Oh!" said Betsy. "You'd better hurry before all the water leaks out."

Soon Billy and Betsy reached Mr. Kilpatrick. He had a group of children around him. "Billy has tadpoles in a box," shouted Betsy.

"Have you, Bill?" cried one the boys. "Let's see them," said another. "What are you going to do with them?"

"Come along, come along," said Mr. Kilpatrick, as he hurried the little group across the street. "We don't want the tadpoles to be late for school."

The whole group rushed into the classroom. "Look, Miss Grey," they cried, "Billy has brought some tadpoles." Billy felt very proud and important as he set the box down on Miss Grey's desk.

"How lovely of you, Billy!" said Miss Grey.

The children gathered around her as she opened the box. "Oh, look!" they cried. "One is bigger than the other." "What are you going to do with them, Miss Grey?"

Miss Grey took a large glass bowl from the shelf in the corner and poured the contents of the box into the bowl. "Now," she said, "we'll add some water and put them on the window-sill. Something very interesting will happen to these tadpoles. We will watch them grow every day."

"We should name them," said Betsy.

"Oh, yes!" cried the children.

"Let's call the little one Wiggle," said Billy.

"Yes," said the children, "let's call him Wiggle."

"And the big one can be Waggle," said Ellen.

So the tadpoles were named Wiggle and Waggle, and the children were delighted.

Every morning they crowded around the bowl to see how the tadpoles were growing. One morning when Betsy reached school she ran to the windowsill. "Oh, Miss Grey," she cried, "something has happened to Waggle. He has two little bumps on each side of his tail." The children came running to look at Waggle. He had, indeed, two little bumps on each side of his tail.

When school began, Miss Grey told the children that the two little bumps were going to be Waggle's legs and that they would grow larger and larger.

"Will Waggle get any more legs?" asked a little boy.

"You wait and see," said Miss Grey.

"I think he will," said Ellen.

"I do too," said Billy.

Sure enough, some time later, two more little

bumps appeared and Waggle began to grow two front legs. Wiggle was very busy growing his back legs and trying to catch up with Waggle.

While the tadpoles were growing their legs, the children were busy learning about the Indians. They learned that there were some Indians who had lived in wigwams made of the skins of animals and some who had lived in wigwams made of birch bark. Miss Grey also told them of Indians who had lived in caves cut in the side of the rocks. The children spent days at the sand table, building an Indian village. They decided to build a wigwam village at one end of the table and a cave village at the other end. They built the wigwam village first. They made the little wigwams of twigs covered with brown paper. They brought little dolls, which they colored with paint.

Betsy thought the Indian village was beautiful. There was even a forest. The trees were made of pieces of sponge painted with green paint. In the middle of the forest there stood a little toy deer. "Because," said Billy, "if there isn't any game the Indians will starve." Billy had learned that animals that are hunted are called "game." He felt very big when he used

this new word because the other children thought that game was just something that you played and sometimes won and sometimes lost.

One morning when the children looked in the bowl to see how Wiggle and Waggle were growing, Waggle looked very strange indeed. "Waggle has lost almost all of his tail," cried Betsy.

"Yes," shouted the children, "look at him, Miss Grey."

"Why, Waggle looks like a frog," said Ellen.

"Waggle is a frog," said Miss Grey. "All this time, Waggle has been turning into a frog." The children laughed. They thought Waggle was wonderful to have turned into a frog.

"He should have a stone to sit on," said a little boy. "Frogs like to sit on stones."

"Yes," said Miss Grey, "and I have had a stone waiting for Waggle." Miss Grey let Billy put the stone in the bowl because Billy had brought the tadpoles to school. The top of the stone stuck up above the water. Later that day, Betsy looked in the bowl and there was Waggle sitting on the stone.

One morning when Miss Grey came into her classroom, Kenny Roberts was alone in the room. He was sitting at his desk busily pasting pictures

in his scrapbook. Kenny had been absent for
several days and Miss Grey had asked him to
come to school early and paste his pictures so
that he would catch up with the other children.

"Good morning, Kenny," said Miss Grey, "you
are a very good boy to get here so early to paste
your pictures."

Kenny said "Good morning" and pounded very
hard on a picture of a horse.

"Do it quietly, Kenny," said Miss Grey.

Kenny was a very small boy. He was like a
little eel for he was never still. His black eyes

were always dancing in his head. When he knew the answer to one of Miss Grey's questions, he would lean way over his desk and shake his hand so hard that Miss Grey thought that some day he would surely shake it off. Kenny always knew the answers. When there was an errand to be done, Miss Grey sent Kenny because he always came back with the right thing.

In a few moments Betsy and Ellen came into the room. "Oh, Kenny," cried Betsy, "did you see Waggle?"

"He is all grown up," said Ellen.

"I'm busy," said Kenny. "I have to paste my pictures."

Betsy and Ellen went to the windowsill and looked in the bowl. "Oh, Miss Grey," cried Betsy. "Waggle is gone!"

Miss Grey left the blackboard where she was drawing a clock and came to the children. Sure enough, Waggle was gone. "He must have jumped out of the bowl," said Miss Grey. The children began looking all around. They looked on the windowsill and on the floor. Kenny stopped pasting pictures and joined the search. As more children arrived they looked for Waggle. They looked on the nearby table and they looked behind the books. They even looked in the waste-paper basket, but Waggle was nowhere in sight. "Oh, dear," said the children, "where could he have gotten to?"

The bell rang for school to begin and the children sat down at their desks. Miss Grey thought she had never seen so many sad little faces before. "Never mind," said Miss Grey, "we won't worry about Waggle. We shall find him for he must be in the room somewhere."

Later in the morning the children went to the sand table to build the Indian cave village. Ellen dipped some water out of the bucket which was under the table. She poured it on the sand. The children began to build the wet sand into a pile. "First we have to make the big rock," said Billy.

"Yes," said Mary Lou, "because the Indians cut the caves out of the rock."

"I'm going to be an Indian when I grow up," said Richard.

"You can't be an Indian," said Ellen.

"Yes, I can," answered Richard.

"You can't be an Indian, because your mother and your daddy are not Indians," said Betty Jane.

"Well, I don't care, I am going to be an Indian

anyway," said Richard, and he patted the sand very hard.

Suddenly one of the little wigwams at the other end of the table jumped up and landed in the middle of the table. "Oh!" squealed the children, and the wigwam jumped again and knocked down an Indian brave and two girls. "Oh! Oh!" squealed the children.

Miss Grey picked up the wigwam and there was Waggle. He hopped all around the village, knocking over more Indians.

Miss Grey caught him and put him back in the bowl. She looked at all the children. When she looked at Kenny, his face grew very, very pink. "Kenny," said Miss Grey, "did you put the little frog under the wigwam?"

Kenny shook his head up and down and wondered how Miss Grey knew that he had hidden Waggle.

"That wasn't like you, Kenny," said Miss Grey.

Kenny's eyes filled with tears, as all of the children looked at him.

"I think Kenny had better sit in the little chair in the corner and do some quiet thinking," said Miss Grey.

Kenny walked to the corner and sat down with his back to the room.

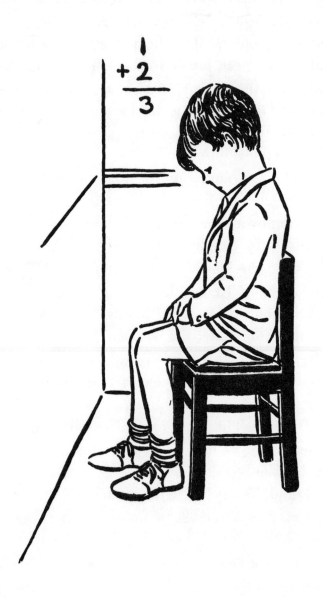

The children were very quiet as they stood the Indians up again and straightened the wigwams. Kenny sniffled and gulped hard. Ellen looked in the bowl. "Oh, Miss Grey," she cried, "Wiggle is sitting on the stone too. Now we have two little frogs."

5

Ellen Has a Birthday

E llen and Betsy were very best friends. They always played together in the schoolyard. Sometimes Ellen would go home with Betsy after school and sometimes Betsy went with Ellen. Betsy lived in a bigger house than Ellen and Betsy had more toys, but Ellen had a baby sister. She was just like a real live doll. Ellen had a grandmother too. She lived at Ellen's house.

Grandmother knew how to make cinnamon buns and always remembered that children like cinnamon buns to be very sticky. So Betsy loved to visit Ellen just as much as Ellen liked to visit Betsy.

One day Betsy and Ellen met at the Good Lady's store. Betsy was buying a red pencil and Ellen was buying a blue one. The Good Lady kept a tiny store right near the school. She sold ice cream and candy, pencils and notebooks, erasers, crayons, and toys. Her name was Mrs. Good, but she was called the Good Lady by all the children because she always made the ice-cream cones stand up like mountains. No child ever bought a pencil or a notebook from her without receiving a peppermint drop or a jelly bean.

The two little girls left the shop together. They were each sucking a peppermint drop. Outside, they stopped to look in the window. The Good Lady's window was always shiny and clean. "Oh, Betsy," cried Ellen, "look at the dear little set of doll's dishes." Right in the center of the window there was a box filled with the prettiest dishes Betsy had ever seen. There were six tiny cups, no bigger than thimbles, and six tiny sau-

cers. There was a little teapot, a sugar bowl, and a cream pitcher. Each piece had a bright pink rose painted on it. They were all carefully packed in pink cotton. "I would love to have those dishes for my birthday," said Ellen.

Ellen's birthday was only two weeks off. Ellen had been talking about her birthday for a long time. It was a very important birthday because Ellen would be six years old. She wished that she could have a party, but Ellen's father worked at night and he had to sleep in the daytime. So the children could never have parties. You couldn't have a birthday party without a donkey game, and you couldn't play a donkey game without making a noise. So Ellen would not be able to have a party. But there would be presents. Ellen said there were always presents even if you didn't have a party.

After school, Betsy stopped at the window again to look at the dishes. How she would love to give those pretty little dishes to Ellen for her birthday! Betsy decided that she would take all of her money out of her bank. She would buy the dishes with the money. Betsy's little bank was a round, fat, yellow duck. He opened his wide bill and swallowed pennies. Betsy called him Big Bill. She wondered whether Big Bill had swallowed enough pennies to pay for the dishes. Father gave Betsy ten brand-new pennies every week. She had been putting half of them in Big Bill. "But now I will put all of them in," thought Betsy. She fed every one of Father's ten pennies to Big Bill. When Mother gave her a penny for candy or a pretzel, Betsy dropped it in her bank. Big Bill grew heavier and heavier. When Betsy shook him he rattled loudly and made Betsy feel very rich. She was sure that she would be able to buy the dishes very soon.

Every day Betsy stopped at the store window to look at the pretty dishes. Two days before Ellen's birthday, Mother drove Betsy to school in the automobile. When Betsy and her mother reached the school, Betsy said, "Mother, please come look at the dear little dishes in the Good Lady's window." Mother was in a great hurry, but she stepped out of the car and went with Betsy to look in the shop window. "Aren't they lovely little dishes, Mother?" asked Betsy. "I want to buy them—"

"Not now," interrupted Mother, "we can talk about them when there is more time. Run along now, Betsy."

Betsy ran along to school and Mother drove away.

That afternoon when school was over, Betsy stopped again to look in the window. The dishes were gone. Betsy couldn't believe her eyes. The dishes had been there this morning and now there was just an empty space. Betsy had never thought that someone else might buy them. She had thought of them always as Ellen's dishes. *Perhaps*, thought Betsy, *The Good Lady still has them inside*. She opened the door of the shop. The sleigh bells, hanging on the door, jingled. Betsy walked up to the counter. The Good Lady smiled and said, "Well, my dear?"

"Where are the little dishes?" asked Betsy, pointing to the window.

"I just sold them an hour ago," said the Good Lady. "Were you thinking of buying them?" she asked. Betsy nodded her head. "Now that's too bad," said the Good Lady. "Perhaps I have something else you would like?" But Betsy did not like anything else. She had set her heart on the dishes for Ellen and now they were gone. Betsy walked home feeling very sad.

When she reached home, Mother was sitting in the library. She was sewing. When she saw

Betsy's sad little face, she said, "Betsy, what's happened to Mother's little Sunshine?"

Betsy ran to Mother. "Oh, Mother," she cried, "the dishes are gone. Now I can't give them to Ellen for her birthday."

Mother lifted her little girl on her lap. "Betsy, darling," she said, "I didn't know that you wanted to give the dishes to Ellen." Betsy hid her face on Mother's shoulder. "Look at Koala over there in the corner," said Mother.

Betsy looked and there sat Koala Bear, having a tea party all by himself. There were the six little cups and saucers, the teapot, the sugar bowl, and cream pitcher all spread out in front of him. Betsy couldn't believe her eyes. "Where did they come from, Mother?" she asked.

"I bought them on my way home," replied Mother. "I thought my little girl wanted them."

"Oh, no," said Betsy, "I wanted to buy them for Ellen with my own money. Big Bill is full of pennies that I have saved."

"Ellen can still have her present," said Mother. "I have saved the box."

"And the pink cotton?" asked Betsy.

"Yes, and the pink cotton," replied Mother.

"Oh, thank you," said Betsy. "It's a lovely present, isn't it, Mother?"

At last Ellen's birthday arrived. It was Saturday. Betsy's mother had invited Ellen and her mother and her baby sister to spend the afternoon. Ellen wore her best dress. It was a white dress with tiny blue forget-me-nots all over it. It had a blue sash. When they reached Betsy's house, Betsy ran to the door to meet Ellen. Betsy handed Ellen the little box and said, "Happy birthday, Ellen." Ellen unwrapped the paper around the box. Betsy held her breath as Ellen took off the lid. Under the lid was a layer of pink cotton. Slowly Ellen lifted one end of the cotton and looked underneath. There was the pink-and-white tea set! "Oh!" said Ellen. "Oh, my little dishes!" Then both Betsy and Ellen began to laugh because they were so happy. Ellen was so excited she forgot to say "Thank you."

After a while, Billy Porter arrived. He had a package for Ellen. When she opened it she found six pretty handkerchiefs. In a few minutes Kenny Roberts came. He had a present for Ellen, too. Then came Mary Lou, and Betty Jane, and Peter, and Christopher. They each had a present for Ellen. Ellen was so surprised and so happy she didn't know what to do, but she did remember

to say "Thank you." When they went into the library and Ellen saw a donkey game pinned on the wall, she cried, "Why, it's a party! I am having a birthday party!"

The children had a merry time trying to pin the tail on the donkey. Billy pinned it right on the donkey's nose. Christopher pinned it on his ear, which made the donkey look very funny indeed. Betty Jane pinned it on the donkey's hind leg, and everyone agreed that Betty Jane had come nearer to putting the tail in the right place than anyone else. So Betty Jane won the prize. It was a box of paints with two brushes and a lot of pictures to color.

After the children had played games, Betsy's mother took them into the playroom. There were a table and eight little chairs. In the center of the table there was a birthday cake. It was covered with white frosting and decorated with pink roses. It had six lighted pink candles. Ellen thought it was the most beautiful birthday cake she had ever seen. The children sat down and Betsy's mother brought them plates of pink ice cream. Then Ellen blew out the candles and cut her cake. She was too little to cut the slices, so Betsy's mother cut each of the children a slice of birthday cake.

That night, when Ellen's father went into her room for a goodnight kiss, Ellen was very sleepy. When her father leaned over her bed, he heard her say, "I had a birthday party. Pink candles and—donkey—tails—and—dishes."

6

Grandma Pretzie

Every morning at recess time an old lady came to the schoolyard gate. The children called her Grandma Pretzie. On one arm she carried a big basket of fresh pretzels, and on the other arm a little stool. She sat on the stool and sold the pretzels for a penny apiece. They were big, thick pretzels, golden-brown, and sprinkled with coarse salt. The children loved the pretzels and they loved Grandma Pretzie. She was very, very old. Betsy thought that she must be a hundred years old, but she really wasn't quite as old as that. She was very poor and she lived in a tiny wooden house near the school. Her face was wrinkled like a dried-up apple. She always wore a little black bonnet that tied under her chin with black ribbons. On very cold days she would pull her woolen shawl up over her head.

Grandma Pretzie knew the most wonderful fairy stories and the children would gather 'round her at recess and shout, "Tell us a story, Pretzie, tell us a story." Pretzie would always say, "Go 'long with you, I don't know any stories today. I have to sell my pretzels." But the children would coax and tease until at last the old lady would begin—"Once upon a time," and she would tell them a story. It was wonderful, the way Pretzie could tell stories and sell pretzels at the same time.

One day in November, Miss Grey told the children that it would soon be Thanksgiving Day. She asked them if they knew what Thanksgiving is. Billy said, "I know, Miss Grey; it's the day you eat turkey." Betsy said it was a day when

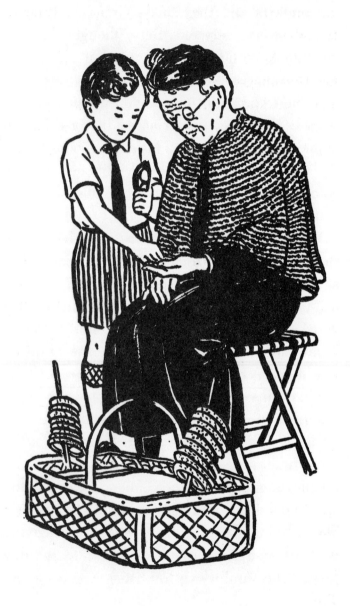

you said thank you to God, and Miss Grey said that Betsy was right.

Then Miss Grey told the children about the first Thanksgiving which was hundreds of years ago. She told them about the people who had come to America from away across the ocean, and how they had to cut down the trees to build their houses and dig big rocks out of the ground before they could plant their seeds. Miss Grey said that these people were called Pilgrims. The Pilgrims were so thankful to God for His care that they decided to have a special day just to say thank you to Him. "And that is the reason," said Miss Grey, "that we have a Thanksgiving Day every year."

Miss Grey asked the children if they would like to fill a basket with food for someone who did not have enough money to buy a Thanksgiving dinner.

"Yes, yes," cried the children.

"I can bring some eggs," said Billy. "My father has chickens and we have lots of eggs."

"Who will we give the basket to?" asked Ellen.

"Let's give it to Grandma Pretzie," said Betty Jane; "she would like to have a Thanksgiving dinner."

"Oh, yes," cried the children, "let's give it to Grandma Pretzie. May we, Miss Grey?"

Miss Grey said that she thought it would be lovely to give a Thanksgiving basket to Grandma Pretzie. "You must not tell her," said Miss Grey, "because it must be a surprise." So it was a big secret.

The children all loved secrets and they loved surprises. They whispered in the schoolyard about Pretzie's basket and what they would put in it. Oh, if they could only have a turkey in the basket! They did wish there could be a turkey.

At home Betsy chatted with Father and Mother about the Thanksgiving basket.

"It's so much fun, Father, to make a basket all full of Thanksgiving," said Betsy.

"It certainly must be," replied Father. "Will there be a turkey in the basket?"

Betsy shook her head and looked very grave. "No," she said. "Miss Grey says that turkeys cost a great deal. She thinks that Grandma Pretzie would like a chicken almost as much as a turkey. But Billy Porter says that Thanksgiving is the day you eat turkey and there ought to be a turkey in the basket. And I think Billy is right."

"Of course he is right," said Father.

"But where can we get a turkey, Father?" asked Betsy.

"Well," said Father, "I don't know, but turkeys are very fond of secrets and surprises. They have a way of popping up when you are not expecting them."

"Do you think one will pop up in Grandma Pretzie's basket?" asked Betsy.

"Now, that I can't say," replied Father, "but I would keep on hoping if I were you. You never can tell about turkeys."

One evening when Father came home, he had two big turkeys with him. "Oh, Father," cried Betsy, "are we going to have two turkeys for our Thanksgiving dinner?"

Father just grinned and made a noise like a turkey, "Gobble, gobble, gobble." He carried the turkeys into the kitchen.

The next morning, when Betsy reached school, she said, "Miss Grey, we have two turkeys at our house. Father brought them home last night."

"How nice!" said Miss Grey.

"Oh, boy," shouted Billy, "you're going to eat plenty of turkey at your house!"

The day before Thanksgiving Miss Grey brought a great big basket to school. It was to hold all

the good things that the children were bringing
for Grandma Pretzie.

Ellen brought a can of soup and Peter brought
cranberries. As each child arrived the pile of
good things on Miss Grey's desk grew bigger and
bigger. There were nuts, celery, potatoes, apples, and oranges. Everything you could think
of for a Thanksgiving basket was there.

Betsy brought a loaf of bread and a pound of
butter. Father drove Betsy to school that morning

because she had so much to carry. Father had a big package all wrapped up in brown paper. "What is in the big package?" asked Betsy.

"Just something I have to leave at the school," said Father, and his eyes twinkled. Betsy knew it was a secret because Father's eyes always twinkled when he had a secret. When they reached the school, Father gave the package to Mr. Windrim, the janitor. Mr. Windrim carried it down to the basement.

Betsy carried her loaf of bread and pound of butter into her classroom and added them to the pile on Miss Grey's desk.

Just before the bell rang, Billy came running in. "Look at Billy's hat," shouted the children.

Billy was wearing his red and blue knitted cap. It was the kind of cap that hangs down the back, like a sock, and it had a tassel on the end. But now the cap stood up straight and stiff on Billy's head. He looked just like the clown in the circus. There was something wet and yellow trickling down Billy's face. "Miss Grey," cried Billy, "something has happened to the eggs."

"Where are the eggs, Billy?" said Miss Grey.

"In my hat," said Billy, pointing to his high cap. "I'm afraid to take it off."

Miss Grey carefully removed Billy's cap. In-side there was a bag of eggs. One egg had broken and was all over Billy's hair.

"Why did you put the eggs in your hat, Billy?" asked Miss Grey.

"I was afraid I would drop them," said Billy.

Miss Grey and all of the children laughed, for Billy looked very funny with the egg all over his face. Miss Grey took him into the cloakroom and washed his hair and face at the sink. The chil-dren were glad Billy hadn't broken all of the eggs. There were still eleven whole ones.

The children helped Miss Grey pack the bas-ket. When all of the things were in the basket, Miss Grey went out of the room. When she re-turned, she was carrying a big turkey.

"Oh," squealed the children, "a turkey! A turkey!" They clapped their hands for joy. "Where did you get it, Miss Grey?" they asked.

"Oh, a little bird brought it," said Miss Grey.

"It must have been a great big bird to carry that big turkey," said Ellen.

Miss Grey laid the turkey right on the top of the basket. It was a beautiful Thanksgiving bas-ket!

At recess, Miss Grey told Grandma Pretzie that the children wanted her to come into their room when the bell rang. The children were so excited they could hardly wait. When the bell rang at the end of recess, they all hurried into the room. In a few minutes, Grandma Pretzie came in. "Betsy," said Miss Grey, "will you tell Grandma Pretzie what we have for her?"

Betsy stood up. "Grandma Pretzie," she said, "we have a Thanksgiving basket for you. We want to give it to you because you are so good to us and tell us stories."

The old lady's eyes filled with tears. "Thank you, my dears," she said, "thank you so much."

The basket was so heavy that Grandma Pretzie couldn't carry it. Mr. Windrim, the janitor, carried it home for her. She carried her pretzel basket and her little stool.

The next day when Betsy was eating her Thanksgiving dinner she suddenly remembered that Father had brought two turkeys home. "Father, where is the other turkey?" asked Betsy.

"That's right," said Father, "there was another turkey. Now where do you suppose that turkey got to?" Father's eyes twinkled, so Betsy was sure that Father knew where the other turkey went.

"Is it a secret?" asked Betsy.

"Yes," said Father, "it's a secret."

7

A Present for Betsy

Curly was a little cocker spaniel. She lived in a house near Betsy's school. Her master was an old gentleman who, Betsy thought, looked the way Santa Claus would look without his whiskers. His name was Mr. Applebee.

Every morning Curly was in the yard in front of her house. She loved to watch the children go by on their way to school. She would run back and forth behind the white picket fence. Her little sharp barks and whines said, "See! See! Here I am. Please play with me. Please!" Many of the children stopped at the fence to look at the little dog. Then Curly would put her front paws up against the fence and stretch her little body until her nose almost touched the children's faces. She would sniff, sniff, sniff, very hard, as though she loved the smell of little children. Sometimes the children would pat Curly's head and her stubby tail would wag with joy.

Betsy loved Curly. Every morning, Betsy stopped at the white fence to see the little dog. She would scratch Curly's head back of her long silky ears. Curly would wag her tail very hard. When Betsy stopped scratching, Curly would poke Betsy's hand with her little wet nose. This was Curly's way of saying, "Scratch some more." Betsy would give her one more scratch and a pat on the head and then run on to school.

One morning, Betsy was walking to school with Christopher. They stopped to see Curly. "Look, Betsy," said Christopher, "I can make her sit up." Christopher pinched up his fingers and made believe that he had something for Curly. "Sit up, Curly! Sit up!" said Christopher. Curly

sat up at once and begged. She sat straight and still with her big soft paws crossed in front of her. She looked very hopeful. "Speak!" said Christopher. "Speak for it!" Curly gave a little sharp bark. Then Christopher opened his hand and there was nothing at all for Curly. She looked so disappointed. Christopher laughed.

"Oh, Christopher," cried Betsy, "you shouldn't make her sit up and not give her anything. You're a very naughty boy."

"Well, I'm glad I'm not a girl," said Christopher, and he pulled one of Betsy's braids and ran off.

Betsy patted Curly's silk head and scratched her ears. "Never mind, Curly, I'll bring you something tomorrow," said Betsy, and she trotted off to school.

That afternoon, when Betsy went home, she climbed up on a chair and took Big Bill off her mantel shelf. Big Bill was very heavy with all the pennies he had swallowed. Betsy took a tiny key from a box on her bureau. She unlocked a door that was hidden under one of Big Bill's wings. She shook out a handful of pennies and closed the little door. Off she ran with the pennies to the corner grocery store.

"Well, Betsy," said the grocer, "what do you want?"

"How much is a box of puppy biscuits?" asked Betsy.

"Ten cents," said the grocer.

"I want a box, please," said Betsy.

She counted out the ten pennies and the grocer gave her a box of biscuits.

"When did you get a dog, Betsy?" asked the grocer.

"We didn't get any," said Betsy, as she closed the shop door.

The grocer chuckled and wondered what Betsy was going to do with puppy biscuits and no dog. But Betsy knew.

The next morning, she tucked a puppy biscuit in the little pocket of her schoolbag. She could hardly wait to see Curly. When she reached the white fence, there was no little black dog running up and down. Betsy looked around the side of the house. Curly was nowhere in sight. She called, "Here, Curly!" but there was no patter of soft paws. The yard looked empty without Curly. *She must be here somewhere*, thought Betsy. *She always is.*

Betsy waited by the fence, hoping that Curly

would appear. She waited until she was afraid she would be late for school. Then she ran as fast as her legs could go. Just as she sat down at her desk, the bell rang. *I'll give Curly the puppy biscuit on the way home,* thought Betsy.

But after school, when Betsy stopped at the fence, the yard was still empty. Again she called, "Here, Curly! Here, Curly!" It was no use. Betsy waited by the fence a long time. All of the other children had gone home but Betsy still waited, hoping that Curly would come out. She did want to give her the biscuit. At last Betsy decided to go home. She would keep the puppy biscuit until tomorrow.

When Betsy reached the wide street, Mr. Kilpatrick was just about to drive away in his police car. When he saw Betsy he got out of the car. "Well, Little Red Ribbons, don't tell me that you were kept after school!" said Mr. Kilpatrick, as he took Betsy across the street.

"No," said Betsy, "I wanted to give Curly a puppy biscuit, but she wasn't in the yard."

"Wouldn't Curly be sorry if she knew that she had missed a free lunch!" said Mr. Kilpatrick.

Betsy trotted along, thinking of Curly. Soon she reached the railroad station. As she walked under the bridge, she heard a whining cry. It sounded like a baby crying. Then she heard a little sharp bark. Betsy stopped and listened. She heard the cry again. Betsy looked around her. There was a dirt road beside her. The road led to the baggage station. Betsy started up the road. The cries grew louder, and the sharp bark sounded just like Curly. Betsy's heart beat very fast. She began to run. Back of the baggage station there was a big open lot. The cries came from somewhere on the lot. In a few moments she came upon a deep pit which had been dug in the ground. There in the bottom of the pit was Curly. "Oh, Curly!" cried Betsy. "How did you get way out here?" Curly gave little yelps and wagged her tail. Betsy stooped down to lift Curly out of the pit. It was so deep, she could not reach the little dog. Then Betsy lay down flat on her stomach. Now she could reach Curly. She took hold of her and lifted her out of the pit. Curly was so happy she rolled over and over. Betsy took the strap off of her schoolbag and hooked it through Curly's collar. Then she started back to the house with the white picket fence.

Betsy wondered how she would ever be able to cross the wide street without Mr. Kilpatrick. "How did you ever get across that big wide street, Curly?" asked Betsy. Curly was busy sniffing the ground.

When they reached the street, there was a lady with a baby carriage, waiting to cross to the other side. When she saw Betsy and the little dog, she said, "You'd better hold on to the baby carriage, little girl." So Betsy held on to the carriage, and the lady and the baby and Betsy and Curly all went safely across the street.

"Thank you," said Betsy, as Curly tugged at the leash.

In a few moments they reached the house where Curly lived. Betsy opened the gate and rang the doorbell. She knew how glad Curly's master would be to see his little dog. When the old gentleman opened the door, Curly jumped up on him. "Curly," cried Mr. Applebee, "where have you been? I have been looking for you all day." Then Betsy told Curly's master of how she had found the dog. Mr. Applebee thanked Betsy over and over again as he patted Curly's head.

"Now," said Mr. Applebee, "I will go with you and take you across the street." Betsy put the strap on her schoolbag while Mr. Applebee got his hat and cane.

Curly followed her master to the gate. She wagged her tail hopefully. "No, indeed, Curly, you can't come," said Mr. Applebee. "You have been far enough today."

Just as the gate closed, Betsy remembered something. She opened the little pocket on her schoolbag and took out the puppy biscuit. "Sit up, Curly," she said. Curly sat up and crossed her paws. "Speak!" said Betsy. Curly gave a sharp bark. Betsy dropped the biscuit and Curly caught it. "I wish I had a little dog just like Curly," said Betsy.

Every morning, after Betsy found Curly, the little dog waited by the fence for her puppy biscuit.

One morning, when Betsy reached the fence, Curly was not there. *I do hope Curly isn't lost again,* thought Betsy.

After school, Mr. Applebee was standing by the gate. "Betsy," he said, "come in and see what Curly has."

Betsy went into the house with Mr. Applebee. He led her back to an outside kitchen. There in a big wooden box lay Curly. Four little black puppies were nursing at her side. There were three black-and-white puppies and one coal black one.

"Oh!" cried Betsy. "The dear little puppies!"

Curly's master lifted them up, one by one. "Curly has four sons," said he. "Which one do you want, Betsy?"

"To keep, for my very own?" asked Betsy.

"Yes," said Mr. Applebee, "it is Curly's present to you for rescuing her from the pit."

Betsy looked at the puppies very carefully. It was hard to decide. At last she said, "I would like to have the little black one because he has such a funny little worry wrinkle between his eyes."

Mr. Applebee explained to Betsy that she would have to leave the puppy with Curly until he was big enough to live without his mother.

Every day Betsy stopped to see her puppy, and every night she told Mother and Father about him. She could not decide what to name him.

At last the day came when Betsy could take him home. Mother called for her after school, and they stopped to get the puppy. Betsy held him in her arms all the way home. When they reached home, Betsy put the puppy down on the playroom floor. He ran all around, sniffing. Then he lay down and thumped his little tail very hard, "Thump! Thump! Thump!"

"Have you thought of a name for the puppy?" asked Mother.

Betsy looked at the puppy very lovingly. "Yes," she said, "Thumpy."

8

How Betsy Went to Pick Violets and Got into Trouble

It was April. Betsy's father and mother had gone away on a trip. They were to be gone for a whole week. Mrs. Beckett, who had been Betsy's nurse when she was a baby, came to stay with Betsy while Father and Mother were away. Betsy loved Mrs. Beckett and thought it great fun to have her come to take care of her. They planned to have a picnic and to go to the zoo, but when the time came it was raining. Rain! Rain! Rain! Betsy was sure she had never seen it rain so hard. Every morning she had to wear her rubbers and raincape and carry her umbrella. She could not go out to play with Thumpy after school, and Mrs. Beckett would not let Thumpy in the house. "He tracks mud all over," said Mrs. Beckett. So Thumpy lay sleeping in his cozy dog box in the yard and Betsy spent the long, dark afternoons wandering from one room to another. "I don't know what to do with myself, Mrs. Beckett," Betsy would say.

"Why don't you color pictures or make your doll a new dress?" Mrs. Beckett would answer.

"I don't want to," Betsy would say. "I just want to play with Thumpy."

On Friday morning, Betsy came down to breakfast feeling cross. It had stopped raining, but the sun was not shining. *Anyway I won't have to wear those old rubbers,* thought Betsy.

"Good morning, Betsy," said Mrs. Beckett, when Betsy came into the kitchen.

"Morning," murmured Betsy. "I don't want any oatmeal."

"Oh, yes!" said Mrs. Beckett. "Come sit down at your table and eat your oatmeal."

"But I don't want any," replied Betsy. "I don't like oatmeal."

"Sit down at your table and eat your breakfast," said Mrs. Beckett very sternly. Betsy sat down very slowly.

"I'll drink my milk," said Betsy.

"And you will eat your oatmeal, like a good girl," said Mrs. Beckett. She poured the cream on Betsy's dish of oatmeal.

Betsy drank her milk and played with the oatmeal. She dug a hole in the center of the oatmeal and watched the milk run down and fill up the hole.

"Betsy, you are going to sit right there until you eat your oatmeal," said Mrs. Beckett. Betsy sat a long time, playing with the oatmeal.

"I'll be late for school," said Betsy. "Mother won't like it if I am late for school."

"Very well," sighed Mrs. Beckett, and she looked out of the window. "You needn't wear your raincape, Betsy, but put on your rubbers."

"I don't want rubbers, Mrs. Beckett," said Betsy. "It isn't raining."

"But the pavements are very damp," said Mrs. Beckett.

"They make my feet hot," said Betsy. She began to cry.

Mrs. Beckett brought the rubbers. "Lift up your foot," said Mrs. Beckett.

"I won't wear those rubbers," cried Betsy. She picked up her schoolbag and ran out the door.

Betsy didn't feel at all happy as she trudged along. There were a great many puddles and her feet began to feel very damp. When she reached the white picket fence, Curly was waiting for her puppy biscuit, but Betsy had forgotten to put it in her schoolbag. It was too late even to stop and scratch Curly's ears. Curly looked disappointed as Betsy hurried by.

At recess time, the sun came out and the children made a great deal of noise in the schoolyard. Ellen had stayed home, so Betsy played with Betty Jane and Mary Lou, but it wasn't as much fun as playing with Ellen. Betsy wished that she had another sandwich. She felt so empty.

After school Betsy started on her way home. She stopped to scratch Curly's ears and pat her head. With Mr. Kilpatrick and a group of children, she crossed the street.

Between the street and the station there was a great big stone house that stood on the top of a hill. It was far back from the street and hidden by great trees. Betsy had never been able to see just what the house looked like. The grounds were surrounded by a low stone wall. Betsy loved to walk on the stone wall, so she scrambled to the top. She looked at the grass. It was fresh and green after the long rain. She saw some violets peeping up between green leaves. *Violets*, thought Betsy. *What fun to pick violets!* Betsy ran over to the little clump of violets and began picking the flowers. There was a little sign sticking in the ground. Betsy could not read the sign but she knew what it meant. It meant that you were not to pick the flowers. Betsy paid no at-

tention, but went right on picking, more and more. Her schoolbag felt heavy, so she took it off and laid it by the trunk of a tree. The further she went the more violets she found. She picked them until she had a large bunch. Then she ran back to the stone wall and started for home.

When Betsy reached the corner of her street, she remembered her schoolbag. She had left it lying under the tree. She turned around and ran all the way back to the stone wall. She climbed up on the wall and ran across the grass. She looked under all the trees where the violets grew. Her schoolbag was not there. Her beautiful plaid schoolbag and her shiny black pencil box! They were gone! *What shall I ever do without them?* thought Betsy.

Betsy hurried home. She was very hungry. She had been so busy picking violets that she had forgotten all about her lunch. When she turned the corner of her street she saw Mrs. Beckett at the front gate. "Where have you been, Betsy?" said Mrs. Beckett. "You are very, very late."

"I stopped to pick some violets," said Betsy.

"And look at your shoes!" cried Mrs. Beckett. "They are covered with mud. You have ruined your new shoes."

Betsy began to cry. "I lost my schoolbag too, and my nice shiny pencil box."

Mrs. Beckett looked very cross as she led Betsy into the house. "Come and have your lunch," she said.

Betsy ate every bit of her lunch. She was so hungry! Every once in a while a big tear would drop on her plate.

After lunch she got undressed and Mrs. Beckett tucked her into bed for her nap. Betsy's eyes were red from crying.

"Mrs. Beckett," said Betsy, "I'm sorry I was a naughty girl."

Mrs. Beckett took Betsy in her arms and the little girl put her head on Mrs. Beckett's big, broad bosom. "It's been an awful day. I spoiled my new shoes and I lost my schoolbag," sobbed Betsy. "I don't like being a naughty girl, Mrs. Beckett."

"I know," said Mrs. Beckett. "You're really a very good little girl, Betsy. You just got out of the wrong side of the bed this morning."

Betsy lifted her head and looked at her little white bed. "Why, I couldn't do that," said Betsy, "because there is only one side to get out of. The other side is against the wall."

"Well, never mind," said Mrs. Beckett. "I know that it will never happen again."

"You won't tell Mother that I was a naughty girl, will you?" asked Betsy.

"No, indeed," said Mrs. Beckett. "I wouldn't think of it."

After Betsy had her nap she played in the yard with Thumpy. She helped Mrs. Beckett set the table for supper and dried the knives and forks and spoons.

The next morning, Betsy woke up very early.

She ran to the window and threw sunflower seeds out to the birds. Then she scrambled back into bed and pulled up the covers. She thought of her schoolbag and of the violets she had picked. Mrs. Beckett had put them in a little bowl. She remembered the sign that was stuck in the ground. *It was wrong to pick violets that belonged to some-one else,* thought Betsy. *I wouldn't like someone to come into my yard and pick my flowers.*

When Betsy went downstairs for breakfast, she said, "Mrs. Beckett, I am going to take those violets back and give them to the lady who lives in the big house."

"Why, Betsy, the violets are all wilted," said Mrs. Beckett. "You can't take them back now."

Betsy drank her milk and ate all of her oatmeal. Then she went out into the little garden. There were pansies growing in the flower beds. Betsy picked a little bunch of pansies. "I am going to take these pansies to the lady," said Betsy.

"Very well," said Mrs. Beckett. "Don't stay too long."

Betsy trotted off with her bunch of pansies. She looked very tiny as she walked through the big gate of the house on the hill. She followed the long drive that led to the big porch. She walked up to the great white door. It had a shiny brass knocker. The knocker was so high, Betsy had to jump to reach it. She jumped several times. At last she managed to raise it a little bit. "Thump!" went the knocker. Betsy waited. In a few moments a man opened the door. "Yes, Miss?" said the man.

"Is there a lady?" asked Betsy.

"Yes, Miss," said the man, "right this way."

The man led Betsy through the big hall and up the widest stairway Betsy had ever seen. He took her into a room filled with sunshine and books. In a chair by the window sat a very old lady. On her snow-white hair she wore a lace cap with a lavender ribbon. She was reading.

"A young lady to see you, Madam," said the man.

The old lady laid down her book and looked at Betsy. "Come in, my dear," she said.

Betsy went up to the chair and held out the pansies. "I brought you these pansies," she said, "because yesterday I picked some of your violets."

"You did?" said the old lady. "Then I suppose that is your schoolbag," she said, pointing to a chair in the corner. "My gardener found it."

"Yes, it is," said Betsy. She was so glad to see her schoolbag again.

"Thank you, dear," said the old lady as she smelled Betsy's pansies. "I like pansies much better than violets."

"Do you?" said Betsy. "I'm glad I brought you pansies."

9

Circuses Are Fun

E arly in the month of May, great big circus
pictures appeared. Gay with colors, they
were pasted on signboards and fences all over
the town. Betsy and her little friends were delighted when they saw the pictures because it
meant that the circus was coming. There was a
picture of ten huge elephants, standing on their
hind legs and raising their great trunks and long

white tusks high in the air. There was one of a beautiful lady. She was dressed all in pink with a tiny ruffly skirt that made Betsy think of her Christmas Fairy dress. The lady was riding on a snow-white horse. Father called her a "bareback rider." When Betsy asked why, Father said it was because the horse didn't wear any saddle. Betsy said that she wanted to be a bareback rider when she grew up, and Father said that would be very nice, because he thought that when he grew up he would be a lion tamer and they could both be in the circus together.

"What will Mother be?" asked Betsy.

"Oh, I think Mother would just love to be the Fat Lady," said Father.

"What about Koala?" said Betsy. "Do you think he will be able to get in the circus too?"

"Yes, indeed," said Father. "The Great Koala! The only Koala bear in captivity! Please do not feed peanuts to Koala."

Betsy laughed and said that she thought circuses were fun.

One morning, Miss Grey asked the children if they knew what was coming to town and they all shouted, "The circus!"

Miss Grey said, "Yes, but it would be nicer if you didn't all shout."

So they all whispered, "The circus."

Nearly all of the children had seen the circus the last time it had come to town. So they had a long talk about the circus. First they talked about the barker. Billy said that the barker is the man who stands outside of the big tent and tells the people what they will see inside.

Betsy told about the bareback rider and Ellen told about the trained seals that play ball and bounce the ball right on the tips of their noses.

They talked about the elephants and the lions, the clowns and the trained dogs. Christopher

said, "I always buy a balloon from the balloon man."

Miss Grey asked the children what else you could buy at the circus and Betty Jane said, "Lemonade," and Kenny said, "Peanuts."

"I wonder," said Miss Grey, "if you boys and girls would like to make believe that you are the animals and the people in the circus and give a performance!"

"Yes," cried the children, "let's give a circus."

"Who will come to see it?" asked Betsy.

"We could invite Miss Foster's class," said Miss Grey. The children were delighted and so it was decided that the first grade would give a circus performance the next morning and invite Miss Foster's sixth-grade boys and girls.

"Kenny," said Miss Grey, "you can be the barker and little Peter can be the balloon man."

"Who would like to take charge of the lemonade and peanuts?" asked Miss Grey. The children's hands waved in the air. Miss Grey selected Betty Jane, and Betty Jane looked all around and grinned.

"The rest of you can be anything you wish," said Miss Grey, "and bring costumes if you have them."

Betsy knew at once what she was going to be. She would bring her Christmas Fairy dress and be the bareback rider. There wouldn't be any white horse but she could stand on a table and bounce up and down on her toes.

The next morning, the children were in school bright and early. Betty Jane and Ellen sliced the lemons and squeezed the juice into a big glass pitcher. Peter sat at his desk and blew up balloons. Miss Grey tied the strings on them. Kenny walked around, looking very important in his father's old felt hat. It was so big it rested on his ears and made them stand out like the handles on a sugar bowl. He bustled the children into the dressing room, where they put on their costumes.

Just then the Taylor twins, Richard and Henry, came running in. "Miss Grey," cried Richard, "we are going to be 'Jumbo the Trained Elephant.' Mother gave us a sheet to wear and we have made a long trunk out of rags."

"Fine!" said Miss Grey. "You will make a wonderful elephant!" She covered the two little boys with the sheet and pinned it in the front and the back. She led them into the cloakroom and the children all cried, "Oh, look at the elephant!"

"Now," said Miss Grey, as the bell rang, "is the lemonade all ready?"

"Yes, it's ready," said Betty Jane.

"Then the performance can begin," said Miss Grey.

Kenny took his place by the door and began to shout, "Come and see the circus! The world's most wonderful circus! Come and see the circus!"

Miss Foster's children trooped in and squeezed themselves into the tiny first grade desks. Peter

went up and down the aisles, crying, "Buy a balloon! Buy a balloon!"

Kenny came into the room. "You will now see Betsy, the world's greatest bareback rider," he cried. Out came Betsy in her Christmas Fairy dress and her white dancing slippers. She climbed up on top of the table and bounced up and down on her toes. Everyone clapped.

"Now you will see the great juggler," cried Kenny. Christopher appeared with two lemons. He threw them up in the air. He caught one and the other fell on the floor, but everybody clapped because they thought that Christopher had done very well to catch one lemon.

"Now, folks," shouted Kenny, "we have Jumbo the Trained Elephant! He does stunts." Out trotted the twins under the sheet. Richard was the head of the elephant and Henry was the tail end. It was really a wonderful elephant, until Henry got so close to Richard that Jumbo began to cave in the middle. The more he caved in the more he looked like a camel. But everyone kept looking at his long trunk and that helped them to remember that he was an elephant.

"Sit up, Jumbo," shouted Kenny. Henry immediately sat on the floor and Richard climbed on a little chair. There was a great deal of clapping.

"Dance, Jumbo," shouted Kenny. Jumbo began to dance. He danced so hard that he stepped on his trunk. Richard fell to the floor and Henry came bursting out of the tail end of the elephant.

There lay Richard, all tangled up in Jumbo's skin. The children laughed and laughed at poor Jumbo. Richard was so sorry that he had spoiled Jumbo that he looked as though he were going to cry. Miss Grey said that she thought that Jumbo should have some lemonade, so Richard

and Henry went over to the lemonade table and Betty Jane gave them each a little paper cup full of lemonade.

"Ladies and gentlemen," cried Kenny, "you will now see the trained lions." Billy Porter walked out, followed by three little girls and two little boys. Billy had a whip and he wore a toy revolver in his belt. He cracked the whip and the little boys and girls got up on five boxes and made believe that they were very fierce lions. Billy held a chair in front of him. He had seen the lion tamer in the real circus hold a chair in front of him. Billy cracked his whip again. The lions roared terrible roars.

At that very moment, through the open window, came a real live monkey. He was wearing a little plaid kilt, a bright red jacket, and a red hat.

"Oh, look at the monkey," cried the children. The lions jumped off their boxes and the lion tamer dropped his chair. The clowns came rushing out of the dressing room. With one leap, the monkey landed on the lemonade table and began cracking peanuts. Betty Jane was frightened and ran to Miss Grey.

"There must be an organ-grinder somewhere," said Miss Grey.

The children were so excited that they forgot all about the circus, but the monkey sat quietly eating peanuts as fast as he could.

Miss Grey looked out of the window and, sure enough, there was an organ-grinder, running through the schoolyard gate. He was shouting, "My monkey! My monkey! I lose my monkey!"

"Your monkey is in here," called Miss Grey. "Come in and get him."

The organ-grinder came running into the classroom. He was hot and angry. "Oh," he cried, "you bad, bad monkey! You run-a away, and now you eat-a da peanuts. I'll beat you."

The monkey jumped from the table and hid in the corner.

"Oh, don't let him beat the monkey, Miss Grey," said Betsy.

"Wouldn't you like to have a glass of lemonade?" Miss Grey asked the organ-grinder.

"Lemonade!" said the organ-grinder. "Yes, thank you very much. I like lemonade."

Miss Grey poured out a glass of lemonade and handed it to him. Then she poured some into the monkey's tin cup and he drank every drop.

"He won't beat the monkey, will he, Miss Grey?" Betsy pleaded.

"No," said the organ-grinder, "I no beat-a da

monkey. All same, he very bad monk, to run away." The organ-grinder smiled and showed his white teeth. "You like me to play some music?" he asked.

"Oh, yes!" said the children.

The organ-grinder began to turn the handle on the organ. As he did so, the monkey came out of the corner and began to dance.

How the children shouted and clapped their hands. When the music was over, the monkey tipped his tiny red hat. Ellen gave him some peanuts and he ran up to the organ-grinder's shoulder.

"Good-bye," said the organ-grinder, as he left the room. "Thank you very much for catch my monkey and give me lemonade."

"Good-bye," the children called.

"Well," said Kenny, "I guess the circus is over."

Miss Foster's children passed out of the room, while the first-graders took off their costumes. When they were all in their seats, Billy said, "It was a real circus, wasn't it, Miss Grey?"

"It certainly was," replied Miss Grey.

Peter was still holding his bunch of balloons. "I sold a balloon," he said. "Miss Foster gave me a penny for it."

10

Betsy Goes to the Farm and Tells Old Ned Some News

The last day of school came on a warm day in June. Betsy was promoted, so were Ellen and Billy, Christopher, Betty Jane, and Mary Lou. Kenny was promoted number one of the boys and Betsy was number one of the girls. All the children felt very big, now that they were in the second grade.

Father had promised Betsy a big surprise if

she was promoted. Betsy could hardly wait for Father to come home. At last she heard his key in the front door. Betsy ran to greet him. "Father," she called, "I'm promoted. I was number one of the girls. I'm in the second grade."

Father picked up his little girl and kissed her. "Hurrah for Betsy!" he cried.

"Have you got my surprise?" asked Betsy.

"Yes, indeed!" replied Father, as he set Betsy down.

Betsy looked in Father's pockets, but there was no package. "Where is it?" she asked.

Father laughed. "Oh, this surprise hasn't any shape," said Father. Betsy and Father always called packages shapes. "But it is a very nice surprise," he said. "You will have to wait until tomorrow morning for it."

In the morning, Father and Mother and Betsy were leaving for Grandfather's farm. Father was driving them to the farm, where Betsy and Mother would stay through the long summer. Father would come every Friday and stay until Sunday.

Betsy loved the farm. There was a pony to ride and trees to climb and a great big barn to play in. There was Old Ned, who took her to the village when he went for groceries and feed.

Sometimes he let Betsy drive the horse. Then there was Linda in the kitchen, Linda who made the big ginger cookies that were always in the center of the breakfast table.

There was only one thing that made Betsy feel sorry about going to the farm. That was Ellen. She would miss Ellen so very much. There were no little girls at Grandfather's, just two little boys who lived across the road.

The next morning, Father had everything packed in the car before breakfast. After breakfast, Betsy and Thumpy got in the back of the car and Mother sat beside Father.

"You haven't forgotten my surprise, have you, Father?" asked Betsy.

"No, indeed," said Father as he started the car.

Betsy wondered what the surprise could be. "What do you think it is, Thumpy?" said Betsy. Thumpy was too busy to think about surprises. He was hanging his head out of the window and letting the wind blow his long ears.

Soon Father slowed down and the car stopped. Betsy looked out of the window. They were in front of Ellen's house. Ellen was standing on the front step. She was wearing her best hat and her coat was over her arm. Beside her was a big traveling bag. "Here they are, Mother," Ellen called through the screen door. Ellen's mother and her brother and her baby sister all came running to the front door. Ellen ran out to the car. Betsy's father got out of the car and picked up the traveling bag.

"Well, Betsy, here is your surprise," he said, as he put Ellen and the bag in the back of the car with Betsy.

"Is Ellen going with us?" cried Betsy.

"Yes," said Mother. "She is going to be with us all summer."

"Oh, Father!" cried Betsy. "It's the best surprise I ever, ever had!"

Ellen's mother kissed her little girl good-bye. "Be a good girl, dear," she said.

"I will, Mummy," said Ellen and she waved her hand to her brother and her baby sister.

Betsy's mother put Ellen's best hat in the paper bag with Betsy's and they started off.

It was a long drive to Grandfather's. The road stretched like a ribbon over the hills and down into the valleys. The children chattered. "I brought my doll, Lydia," said Ellen. "I washed all of her clothes and ironed them myself."

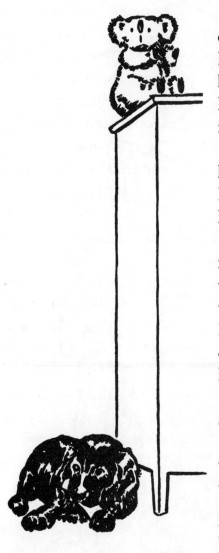

"I brought my doll, Judith," said Betsy. "I couldn't bring Evelyn. Evelyn's eyes fell inside of her."

"Didn't you bring Koala Bear?" asked Ellen.

"Of course," replied Betsy. "I wouldn't go away without Koala Bear. He would cry if I left him all by himself."

"Where is he?" asked Ellen.

"He's riding on the front seat between Father and Mother. Koala likes to ride on the front seat. He likes to see things before he comes to them."

This was only one reason why Koala liked to

ride on the front seat. The other reason was that Thumpy liked Koala better than Koala liked Thumpy. Thumpy liked Koala so much that he loved to play with him, but Thumpy's idea of playing was to shake Koala very hard and then chew him. Koala didn't like it a bit because he couldn't shake and he couldn't chew. So Betsy bought Thumpy a rubber bone, and Koala never sat on the floor but on the tops of things.

"Oh, there is a white cow," cried Betsy, pointing out of the window.

"There's another one," cried Ellen.

The children decided to play a game. They called it "White Cow." Betsy looked out of one window and Ellen looked out of the other window. When Betsy saw a white cow on her side of the road she would call out "White Cow"; and when Ellen saw one on her side she would call out "White Cow." Mother kept the score. By the time they reached the farm, Betsy had seen twenty white cows and Ellen had seen thirty-two. So Ellen won the game.

Grandfather's farmhouse was built on the side of a hill. It was made of stone and had a big porch. The porch ran across the front of the house and around the side. Grandfather called it "the piazza." A trumpet vine ran all over the porch railing and climbed up the posts. Betsy loved the big red trumpet flowers. She was sure the fairies blew them at night and made music.

Grandfather was standing on the front steps when the car drove up the driveway. He opened the car door and kissed Mother and Betsy and shook hands with Father.

"Grandfather, I counted twenty white cows," said Betsy. "But Ellen won because she counted thirty-two."

"Well, well," said Grandfather. "I am glad to see you, Ellen. I didn't know that such little girls could count."

Betsy and Ellen laughed. "Of course we can count," said Betsy. "We go to school. We got promoted too."

"We are in the second grade now," said Ellen.

"My! My!" said Grandfather. "Now I suppose you will be counting my chickens before they are hatched."

Betsy thought for a moment, then she said, "You can't count the chickens before they're hatched, Grandfather. But we'll help you count them after they're hatched."

Grandfather said that dinner was all ready. The children washed their hands and faces and ran to the dining room. Linda was standing by the kitchen door. Her face was shining. Betsy rushed up to Linda. "Hello, Linda. This is Ellen," said Betsy. "She is going to stay all summer. Are there any ginger cookies?"

"Well, I shouldn't be surprised if there were a few," said Linda. "I set a table over here in the corner for you children."

Betsy and Ellen sat down at the little table. It was covered with a red-and-white checked tablecloth. In the center of the table was a plate of big, round, ginger cookies. Betsy's eyes danced when she saw the cookies. "Oh, Linda!" she

cried. "Ginger cookies! And we don't have to wait until breakfast!"

"No," said Linda, "this is special."

After dinner, the children went upstairs to their bedroom. It was a big room with two beds, one for Betsy and one for Ellen. While Betsy and Ellen got ready for their naps, Mother put their clothes away in a big high chest.

The little girls lay down and soon they were fast asleep.

When Betsy woke up, she heard Old Ned's voice under the window. He was talking to Grandfather. Betsy ran to the window. "Oh, Ned," she cried, "are you going to the village?"

"Yes," said Old Ned, "goin' into the village fer oats."

"Can we go with you?" asked Betsy.

"Reckon so," said Old Ned.

Betsy and Ellen scrambled into their new overalls and dashed down the stairs.

"Mighty pretty little girls!" said Old Ned as he lifted them into the wagon. Old Ned picked up the reins. "Gee up, Priscilla," he said. The horse started off down the road.

"Well," said Old Ned, "I hear you been goin' to school."

"Yes," said Betsy, "and we got promoted. We're in the second grade. Ned, you were wrong about school. School is nice, Ned. We love our teacher. She's just sweet. And there isn't any switch, Ned. You said there was a switch." Betsy laughed. "Oh, school is fun! Isn't it, Ellen?"

"Yes," said Ellen. "We built a farm out of wooden boxes and we sawed out the doors and the windows."

"And Billy made a chicken coop," said Betsy.

"Christopher and I made a stable with stalls for the horses," said Ellen.

"Yes, and there was a pigsty and window boxes on the windows of the farmhouse," said Betsy. "I painted them green and Miss Grey gave me some little flowers to put in them. Oh, it was fun!"

"And we had a play at Easter," said Ellen. "Kenny Roberts was a bunny rabbit. He was dressed up in a white bunny suit and his ears fell off."

Ellen and Betsy laughed loudly as they remembered how funny Kenny had looked without his ears.

"Please, may I drive Priscilla, Ned?" asked Betsy. Old Ned handed the reins to Betsy.

"So school is fun!" said Old Ned. "You build farmhouses and chicken coops and dress up like bunny rabbits. Well, well," said he, and he stroked his grizzly beard.

"Yes, school is lovely," said Betsy. "Gee up, Priscilla!"

Turn the page for a peek at Betsy's adventures in

Betsy and Billy

when Betsy and her friends go into second grade.

1

Betsy Goes Back to School

I t was September and vacation days were almost over. Soon it would be time for Betsy to go back to school. She had tried on all of her school dresses that she had worn the year before. Betsy had grown so tall that Mother had to let down all of the hems.

One day Mother was busy hanging the skirt of one of Betsy's dresses. Betsy was standing on a chair. She turned very slowly while Mother put the pins in the skirt.

"Betsy, what are you looking so sober about?" asked Mother.

"I was thinking," replied Betsy.

"And what were you thinking about?" asked Mother.

"I was thinking about school," answered Betsy. "Do you know, Mother, I don't know whether I am going to like being in the second grade."

"Of course you are going to like being in the second grade," said Mother.

"But, Mother, Miss Grey won't be there," said Betsy. "Miss Grey was such a nice teacher. I don't think I am going to like my new teacher. Her name is Miss Little. She isn't pretty like Miss Grey."

"Well, dear, everyone can't be as pretty as Miss Grey," said Mother.

"But Miss Little wears black dresses all the time, Mother," said Betsy. "I used to see her last year and she always had on a black dress. I don't like black dresses. Miss Grey wears pretty dresses, pink ones and green ones and red ones, and once she had a dress that had flowers all over it."

"It has been a long time since school closed," said Mother; "perhaps Miss Little has bought herself some new clothes."

"Well, I hope so," said Betsy.

"Run along now," said Mother, as she helped Betsy down from the chair.

Betsy ran along, but she kept thinking about Miss Little. She began to feel sorry that she had been promoted. *Perhaps I could go back to the first grade*, she thought. But she knew that she wouldn't like that either because she wouldn't know anyone in the first grade. All of her friends were in the second grade. There was her best friend, Ellen, and there was Billy Porter. Betsy chuckled when she thought of Billy. He was such a funny little boy, always calling out from his seat and getting into trouble. Then there were Kenny Roberts and Betty Jane and Mary Lou and the twins, Richard and Henry. She would be so glad to see them all. She would even be glad to see Christopher who sometimes pulled her braids. Betsy could see that she could never give up being in the second grade. She would have to be in Miss Little's room and put up with the black dresses. *Perhaps she hasn't any money to buy pretty dresses*, thought Betsy. And then she began to feel very sorry for Miss Little because she didn't have any money to buy pretty dresses.

One afternoon, Mother cleaned out her closets. She had decided to give away all of her old dresses that she did not wear any longer. At the end of the afternoon she had a big pile of dresses on the bed. She decided to give them to Milly, the laundress. When Betsy saw the pile of dresses, she said, "Mother, may I have some of these dresses to play 'Dress-up Lady'?"

"I think you may," said Mother.

"Oh, Mother," cried Betsy, "may I have this flowered one?" Betsy picked up a flowered silk dress that had been her favorite dress of Mother's.

"Yes," said Mother, "and you may have the red one with the long train. You will be a very grand lady in that dress."

Betsy carried her new treasures off to her own room. She tried them on and paraded up and down the hall. Every few minutes she stopped to look in the mirror. This was a lovely new game and for several days she wore Mother's old dresses almost all of the time. When Ellen came to play with her they each put on one of the dresses. They played that they lived in separate corners of the playroom and they paid calls on each other, and talked about their children.

The day before school was to open, Betsy was wearing the red silk dress. All of a sudden, she thought of Miss Little and her black dresses. Then Betsy had an idea. She took off the red dress and laid it on the bed. Then she pulled the flowered silk one out of the bottom drawer of her bureau. She looked at them very carefully. They were a little mussed and a little soiled around the bottom, but Betsy thought they really looked very nice. She tried to smooth out the wrinkles and all the time she had wrinkles in her forehead, for it was very hard to decide which dress she could part with. She loved them both very much, but she had decided to give one of the dresses to Miss Little. First she thought she would give her the flowered one, but she ended by thinking the red one would be best. Miss Little would look nice in the long train. Betsy folded the dress as carefully as she could and put it in her schoolbag.

The next morning, just as she was leaving for school, Mother said, "Betsy, whatever is in your schoolbag that makes it look so fat?"

"Oh, that is your red dress," replied Betsy.

"I am going to give it to Miss Little so that she will have a pretty dress to wear to school."

"Betsy, darling!" cried Mother. "You can't give that dress to Miss Little."

"Why not?" asked Betsy, looking very crest-fallen. "It's a present for her."

"You can't give dresses to your teacher, dear," explained Mother. "You can give her flowers or candy or fruit and many other things, but not dresses."

Betsy looked puzzled but she opened her schoolbag and pulled out the dress. Mother hugged her little girl very tight when she kissed her good-bye.

Betsy trotted off to school thinking it was very strange that dresses couldn't be presents. Soon she met some of her little friends. They chattered about their summer vacations all the way to school.

When they reached the big wide street, there was Mr. Kilpatrick, the policeman. When he saw the group of children, he blew his whistle and all of the automobiles stopped. The children ran toward the big policeman, calling, "Hello, Mr. Kilpatrick."

Mr. Kilpatrick laughed and shouted, "Hello, there, everybody! Hello, Billy. How are you, Teddy? Why, there's Little Red Ribbons!" Mr. Kilpatrick always called Betsy "Little Red Ribbons" because she often wore red ribbons on her braids.

The children swarmed around the policeman. "Mr. Kilpatrick," shouted Betsy, "I can milk a cow!"

"You don't say so!" said Mr. Kilpatrick.

"Our cat has kittens, Mr. Kilpatrick," said Teddy.

"Look, Mr. Kilpatrick," cried Billy, "I have a loose tooth."

"Run along, run along," shouted Mr. Kilpatrick, as he hustled the children on.

When the children reached the school they trooped into the second-grade room. To Betsy's surprise, Miss Little wasn't there. Instead, the school secretary was standing at the front of the room. "Just take your seats quietly, children," she said. "Your teacher will be here in a few minutes. Miss Little is not coming back to school."

Betsy wondered who her teacher would be. She saw Miss Grey pass the door. She was so glad to see Miss Grey again. It was all she could do to keep from running after her. She began again to wish that she could go back to the first grade with Miss Grey. Betsy could feel a little lump in her throat. She swallowed hard but it didn't do any good. Just as the tears were beginning to come into her eyes, the door opened and in came Miss Grey. "Good morning, boys and girls," said Miss Grey.

"Good morning, Miss Grey," the children said.

"I have a surprise for you," said Miss Grey.

The children's eyes were very wide, for they loved nothing better than surprises.

"I have been promoted," said Miss Grey. "I am in the second grade, too."

"Whoopee!" shouted Billy Porter.

CAROLYN HAYWOOD (1898–1990) was born in Philadelphia and began her career as an artist. She hoped to become a children's book illustrator, but at an editor's suggestion, she began writing stories about the everyday lives of children. The first of those, *"B" Is for Betsy*, was published in 1939, and more than fifty other books followed. One of America's most popular authors for children, Ms. Haywood used many of her own childhood experiences in her novels. "I write for children," she once explained, "because I feel that they need to know what is going on in their world and they can best understand it through stories."